La jornada escolar de Peppa

Peppa's School Day

Adaptado por Meredith Rusu
Adapted by Meredith Rusu

SCHOLASTIC INC.

Originally published in English as Scholastic Reader: *Peppa Pig: Peppa's School Day*

Translated by Eida de la Vega

This book is based on the TV series *Peppa Pig*. *Peppa Pig* is created by Neville Astley and Mark Baker. Peppa Pig © Astley Baker Davies/Entertainment One UK Limited 2003.

ISBN 978-1-338-15902-8

10 9 8 7 6 5   18 19 20 21

Printed in the U.S.A.   40
First Scholastic bilingual printing 2017

Hoy Peppa va a la escuela.

Peppa is going to school today.

¡Todos sus amigos están ahí!

All of her friends are there!

—Hoy tenemos una nueva estudiante —dice la señora Gacela—. Es la elefanta Emily.

"Today we have a new student," says Madame Gazelle. "This is Emily Elephant."

Emily es tímida.
No sabe qué decir.

Emily is shy.
She does not know what to say.

¡Todos están muy contentos de conocer a Emily!

—¿Puedo enseñarle a Emily cómo hacemos mostrar y contar? —pregunta Peppa.

Everyone is excited to meet Emily!

"Can I show Emily how we do show-and-tell?" Peppa asks.

—Por supuesto —dice la señora Gacela.

Peppa le cuenta a la clase sobre su osito de peluche.

"Of course," says Madame Gazelle.

Peppa tells the class about her teddy bear.

Después, es tiempo libre.

Next, it is free time.

—¿Qué quieres hacer hoy?
—le pregunta Peppa a Emily.

"What would you like to do today?" Peppa asks Emily.

Hay pintura, plastilina o bloques.

There is painting, clay, or building blocks.

¡Emily elige los bloques!

Emily chooses building blocks!

Peppa le enseña a Emily a apilar los bloques.

Peppa shows Emily how to stack the blocks.

—Pones uno encima de otro —dice Peppa.

"You put one on top of another," says Peppa.

—¿Así? —pregunta Emily.
—¡Caramba! —dicen los niños.

"Like this?" asks Emily.
"Wow!" say the children.

¡La elefanta Emily coloca muy
bien los bloques!

Emily Elephant is good at
stacking blocks!

¡Luego, es hora de jugar!
—Vamos, Emily —grita Peppa.

Next, it is playtime!
"Come on, Emily," shouts
Peppa.

—¡Durante la hora de jugar, salimos! —dice la gata Candy.

"At playtime, we go outside!" says Candy Cat.

Todos los niños salen corriendo.

All the children run outside.

Primero, se deslizan por el tobogán.

First, they go down the slide.

¡Juiiiii!

Wheeeee!

Luego, se ponen a jugar.
—¿Quién hace el sonido más
alto? —pregunta Peppa—. ¡Oinc!

Then they play a game.
"Who is the loudest?" asks
Peppa. Snort!

¡Oinc!
Snort!

Todos hacen sonidos.
¡Qué alboroto!

They all make loud sounds.
What a lot of noise!

¡¡Prrrrruuu!!
Erowrrhhh!!

—Emily, ahora te toca a ti
—dice Peppa. Emily hace un
sonido como el de una trompeta.

"Emily, you try," says Peppa.
Emily makes a noise like a
trumpet.

¡Ella suena más alto que todos!

She is the loudest of all!

—¿Puedes darle vueltas al aro?
—le pregunta la oveja Suzy a
Emily.

"Can you spin the hula hoop?"
Suzy Sheep asks Emily.

Emily puede darle vueltas al aro.
¡Sabe hacer muchas cosas bien!

Emily can spin the hula hoop.
She is good at lots of things!

Pero todavía queda un juego
por jugar.

But there is still one game left
to play.

—Mi juego preferido es saltar en charcos de lodo —dice Peppa.
—¡Ese también es mi juego preferido! —grita Emily.

"My favorite game is jumping in muddy puddles," says Peppa.
"That is my favorite game, too!" shouts Emily.

Peppa y Emily están contentas de ser amigas.
¡Qué día de escuela tan agradable!

Peppa and Emily are so happy they are friends.
What a nice day at school!